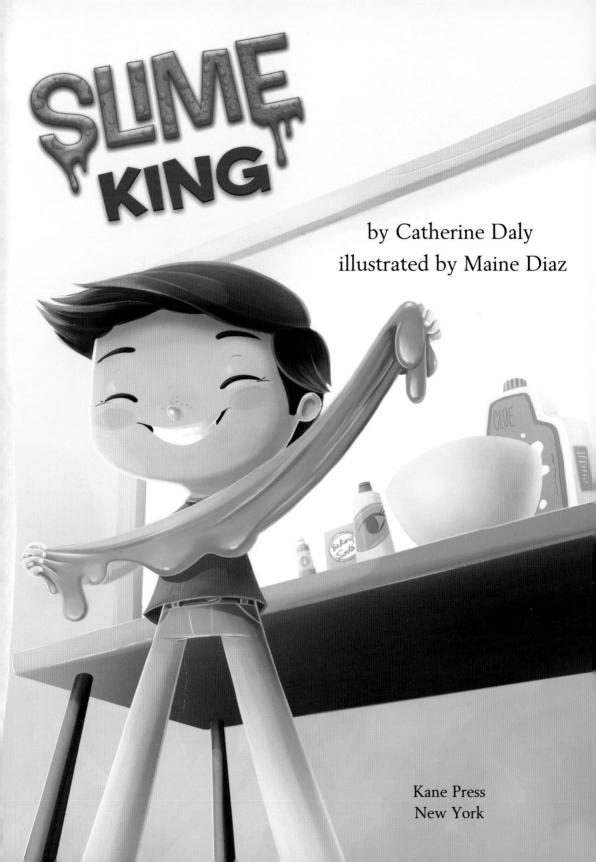

SLIME KING

by Catherine Daly
illustrated by Maine Diaz

Kane Press
New York

Special thanks to Melanie Meade, Education Coordinator of South Fork Natural History Museum, for her slime help.

To the real Oonagh, Slime Queen Extraordinaire, and also to the real Grandpa George, the best science project helper ever.—C.D.

For all those kings who teach us through life.—M.D.

Library of Congress Cataloging-in-Publication Data
Names: Daly-Weir, Catherine, author. | Diaz, Maine, illustrator.
Title: Slime King / by Catherine Daly ; illustrated by Maine Diaz.
Description: New York : Kane Press, 2019. | Summary: Leo has his own slime-making business, but will that help bring his science grade up?
Identifiers: LCCN 2018023102 (print) | LCCN 2018029177 (ebook)
| ISBN 9781635921236 (ebook) | ISBN 9781635921229 (pbk) | ISBN 9781635921212 (reinforced library binding)
Subjects: | CYAC: Toys—Fiction. | Chemistry—Fiction. | Schools—Fiction.
Classification: LCC PZ7.D16945 (ebook) | LCC PZ7.D16945 Sli 2019 (print) | DDC [E]—dc23
LC record available at https://lccn.loc.gov/2018023102

10 9 8 7 6 5 4 3 2 1

First published in the United States of America in 2019 by Kane Press, Inc.
Printed in China

Book Design: Michelle Martinez

Makers Make It Work is a registered trademark of Kane Press, Inc.

Visit us online at www.kanepress.com

Like us on Facebook
facebook.com/kanepress

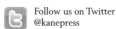
Follow us on Twitter
@kanepress

Leo wore many different hats. Literally.
On Mondays he wore his baseball cap, for practice with his Little League team, the Sebago Stinkbugs.

He wore a chef's hat on Tuesdays.

A helmet on Wednesdays.

A top hat on Thursdays.

And a golf cap on Fridays.

Leo liked all his hats. But there was one that he loved most of all—his golden crown. That's because on weekends he became . . .

The Slime King!

Leo loved making slime. He enjoyed lining up everything that went into the slime. He liked trying new things to come up with the perfect mix. He lived for the moment when it went from a bowl of random stuff to smooth elasticy slime.

And nothing felt as good as the squooshy squishing sound the slime made when you squeezed it just so.

He even had his very own website. . . .

Slime is a non-Newtonian fluid— a liquid that also acts like a solid. Ketchup is also a non-Newtonian fluid.

Slime King

My name is Leo and I am eight years old and I ❤ SLIME! Here you can learn all about the different kinds of slime. You can get recipes and ideas. And you can watch me in action!

SLIME BASICS:

that's my favorite activator!

Non-toxic glue
(white or clear)

Saline solution
& baking soda

Water

Food coloring
(any color you like)

Popsicle sticks
(for stirring)

Plastic bowls
(for mixing your slime in)

Plastic containers
with lids or plastic bags
(for storing your slime)

In 1976, an American toy company came out with a new toy—slime! It was bright green and came in a little trash can.

SLIME TYPES:

 Classic slime (smooth and stretchy)

 Glitter slime (add glitter—duh!)

 Rainbow slime (for best results make each color separately, then swirl together)

 Fluffy slime (add shaving foam)

 Glow-in-the-dark slime (add glow-in-the-dark paint)

 Butter slime (add soft clay)

 Crunchy slime (add sequins, beads, tiny plastic toys, googly eyes, etc.!)

 Color-changing slime (add special powder)

 Sand slime (add craft sand)

 Snow slime (add instant snow)

On Sundays, when Leo's newest slimes were done, Grandpa George filmed him . . .

Kneading the slime.

Poking it.

Pulling it.

Twisting and squishing it.

Rolling and folding it.

Twirling and swirling it.

Sinking his fingers deep into it.

Cutting it.

And making gross noises with it!

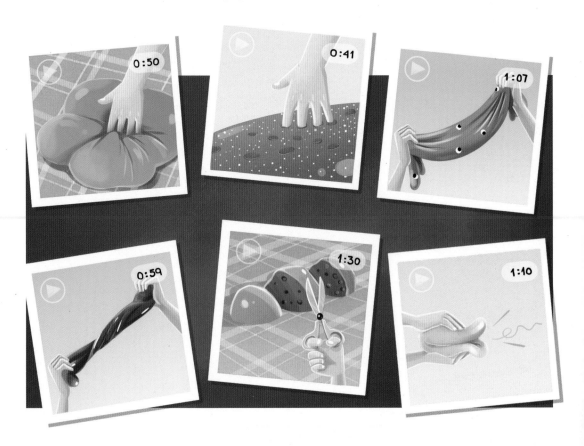

Leo ended each video with his favorite trick—the giant slime bubble. His skills were perfect. (It said so in the comments.)

Leo posted a new video every week. He had 212 followers. And that didn't even count his mom, dad, and Grandpa George.

Leo's parents didn't mind his slime-making as long as he kept his grades up.

That was easy for Leo, for the most part. But he struggled with one subject—science. Nothing about the steps of the water cycle or facts about fossil fuels interested him. It just didn't feel real.

MS. HASSAN

WELCOME, SCIENTISTS

When Leo got to the schoolyard on Mondays, customers were always lined up.

"Hey, I saw your video last night," said Oona. "I'll take one glow-in-the-dark and two unicorn glitter slimes, please."

"Three fluffy slimes for me," said Max. He and was Leo's best customer. "With googly eyes this time. Purple, please."

"The eyes or the slime?" asked Leo.

"Both!" replied Max.

"How did you have time to make all that awesome slime?" asked Andrew. "I was working on our extra credit project all weekend."

Leo froze. "Um . . . what extra credit project?"

"For science, silly," said Andrew.

Leo's stomach sank. He had bombed the last science test, and extra credit was exactly what he needed. Without it, his grade might not be slime-worthy.

He kind of remembered Ms. Hassan saying something in class on Friday. But he had been thinking about what color glitter to put into his unicorn slime recipe. Maybe he hadn't exactly been paying attention.

In science class, Leo watched his classmates present their projects.

Andrew had made a battery out of a pear.

Oona had put food coloring into vases to show how flowers absorb water.

Evan had tested which bounced higher—a bowling ball or a soccer ball.

Sure, some projects were better than others. But they were all getting extra credit. And Leo wasn't.

TODAY'S
EXTRA CREDIT

After the last student was done, Ms. Hassan stopped by Leo's desk. "Do you have anything to share?" she asked.

Leo couldn't look into her warm brown eyes and tell a lie. So he stared at the classroom floor as he fibbed.

"Um . . . I left it at home," he mumbled. Luckily, at that moment the bell rang.

But then Ms. Hassan said the dreaded words. "Leo, will you stay after class for a minute?"

Ms. Hassan walked him to the hallway.
"Leo, you're such a smart boy," she said. "I don't
understand why you have so much trouble in
my class."

"I guess I'm just not a scientist," he replied.

"We are all scientists," said
Ms. Hassan. "Every day."

Leo shook his head. "Not me."

A fifth-grader passed by. "Hey, Slime King!" he called. "Can I put in an order for crunchy slime? I need it for my birthday."

"No problem!" said Leo.

"Slime King?" Ms. Hassan asked.

"Leo makes the best slime ever," said the boy. "You should check out his website!"

Ms. Hassan smiled. "I might do that." She turned to Leo. "Just show up tomorrow. We'll deal with your extra credit then."

Leo wasn't sure why he had gotten off so easily.

That evening he started to worry.

"Why aren't you eating, Leonardo?" Grandpa George asked at dinner. "I made your favorite!"

Leo shrugged.

Leo showed up to science class the next day, feeling nervous.

"Good morning, class," said Ms. Hassan. "Today we'll be seeing Leo's extra credit project. He is going to teach us all about chemistry!"

Leo's heart skipped a beat. "I'm wh-wh-what?" he stammered.

Chemistry is the study of how and why substances combine, separate, and react.

Ms. Hassan called him up to the front of the room. She stood next to a table covered by a sheet. Ms. Hassan winked at Leo. Then she pulled off the sheet. Glue, saline solution, baking soda, a bowl, popsicle sticks, and even food coloring sat on the table. All of Leo's favorite things!

He looked at his teacher.
"I'm going to make slime?"
he asked her.

Ms. Hassan smiled. "You're
going to make slime!" she said.

Leo opened the glue and poured it in the bowl.

"Glue is a polymer," Ms. Hassan explained to the class. "A polymer is a big molecule. It's made up of millions of smaller molecules that are all attached to each other. The glue flows because the molecules slide past each other."

Polymer comes from the Greek words "poly" and "mer" meaning "many parts."

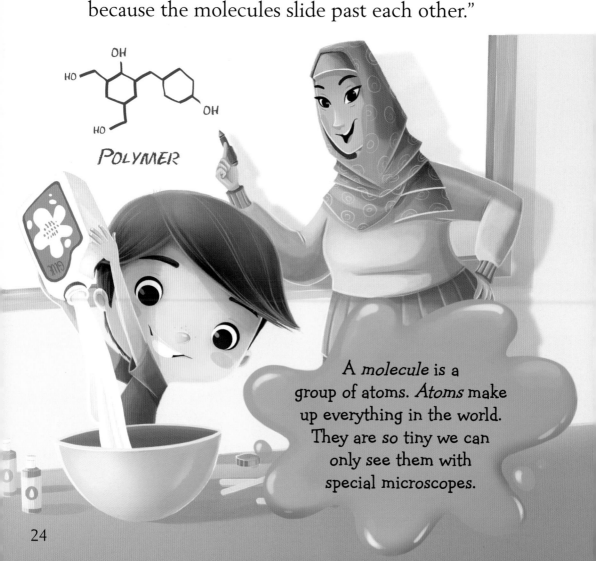

POLYMER

A *molecule* is a group of atoms. *Atoms* make up everything in the world. They are so tiny we can only see them with special microscopes.

Leo added some water to the glue. Then he added baking soda.

"Ms. Hassan, what's your favorite color?" he asked.

"Green," she answered.

Leo grinned. "I should have guessed."

He added a couple drops of green food coloring and stirred. Then he picked up the saline solution.

"This is the activator," Leo told the class. He squirted saline solution into the bowl. As he stirred, the mixture began to thicken.

All of a sudden Leo realized what was happening. "Hey, the saline solution is making a chemical reaction with the glue!" he cried.

A slime *activator* is the liquid that's added to the glue to connect the molecules. This changes the glue into slime.

Ms. Hassan beamed. "Why yes, it is!" she said. "The borate in the saline solution is causing the structure of the glue to change. The polymers aren't sliding anymore. They're sticking together."

CHEMISTRY

Leo's favorite activator is saline solution. Other activators are liquid starch, laundry detergent, or borax powder plus water. These all contain a chemical compound called *borate*.

Andrew called out, "Make special glitter slime for Ms. Hassan!" So Oona ran to the art room and came back with some glitter. Leo mixed it in and gave it to his teacher.

"Wow!" she said. "It's so beautiful. You *are* the Slime King!"

"Next time I'll wear my crown," he said.

Ms. Hassan held up the slime to the class.
"And that's it," she said. "The science of slime!"
Leo stood in front of the class, a big grin on
his face. Ms. Hassan was right. He *was* a scientist.
Who knew he had been one all along!

After that, Leo not only got a good grade in science on his next report card . . . he also got a new customer!

Learn Like a Maker

A chemist is a scientist who experiments with chemicals and their reactions. Start with a polymer (glue), mix in some basic chemicals (water and baking soda), add an activator (saline solution), and you can be a chemist, too!

Look Back

- On page 18, Ms. Hassan says, "We are all scientists. Every day." Do you agree with her? What is one way you're a scientist?

- Speak like a scientist! After reading pages 26–27, look at the definition of "activator." Use your own words to summarize what this term means. Why is an activator important to the process of making slime?

Try This!

Make Your Own Slime!

You will need:

- a 4-ounce bottle of white washable school glue
- ½ cup of water
- ½ – ¾ teaspoon of baking soda
- 1 tablespoon of contact lens solution (saline solution)

In a large bowl combine the water with the glue. Then stir in the baking soda. Finally, add the contact lens solution and mix well.

Change it up. Instead of ½ cup of water, try 3 cups of shaving cream. How does that change the feel of the slime? Which type of slime do you like better?

Make it unique. You can add food coloring or glitter, or try something else to make your slime special!